The Four Ugly Cats in Apartment 3D

The Four Ugly Cats in Apartment 3D

illustrations by

ROSANNE LITZINGER

ALADDIN PAPERBACKS
NEW YORK   LONDON   TORONTO   SYDNEY   SINGAPORE

First Aladdin Paperbacks edition October 2003

ALADDIN PAPERBACKS
An imprint of Simon & Schuster Children's Publishing Division
1230 Avenue of the Americas, New York, NY 10020

Also available in a Richard Jackson Books,
Atheneum Books for Young Readers hardcover edition.
Designed by Michael Nelson
The text of this book was set in Esprit.

Printed in the United States of America
2 4 6 8 10 9 7 5 3 1

The Library of Congress has cataloged the hardcover edition as follows:
Sachs, Marilyn.
The four ugly cats in apartment 3D / Marilyn Sachs.
p. cm.
"A Richard Jackson book."
Summary: After a neighbor in her apartment building dies, ten-year-old Lily tries to find homes for his four ugly, noisy cats.
ISBN 0-689-84581-2 (hc.)
[1. Cats—Fiction. 2. Neighbors—Fiction. 3. Apartment houses—Fiction.]
I. Title.   PZ7.S1187 Fm 2002
[Fic]—dc21   00-200140225
ISBN 0-689-86353-5 (Aladdin pbk.)

*For my niece, Carol,
whose love inspired this book*

The Four Ugly Cats in Apartment 3D

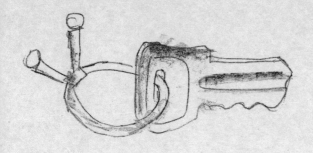

Mr. FREEMAN IN APARTMENT 3D was nice to me once.

That was a year ago, when I was ten. My name is Lily. I take care of myself when my mother is working. Which is most of the time.

I didn't know that day about my key until I arrived home from school. I looked for it in my backpack. It wasn't in my backpack. I looked for it in my coat pocket. It wasn't in my coat pocket. It was still inside on the kitchen table.

I rang Mrs. Hernandez's bell in 3A. She always says I can ring her bell if I need anything. Sometimes she gives me milk and cookies even if I don't need anything. Mrs. Hernandez wasn't home.

Then I rang Mr. Kaspian's bell in 3C. He isn't as friendly as Mrs. Hernandez. But he isn't unfriendly, either. He didn't answer. I rang it again. He still didn't answer.

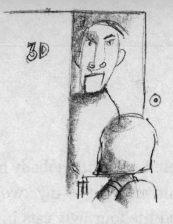

The only other person on our floor was
Mr. Freeman in 3D. But I never for a
moment thought of ringing Mr. Freeman's
bell. Mr. Freeman was mean, unfriendly,
and nasty. He was also loud, especially
when he argued with Mrs. Hernandez or
Mr. Kaspian. He was ugly, too. And he
had four ugly cats who were just as loud
as he was. You could hear them yowling
any time you stood outside on our floor.
Day or night. Like that very minute.

So there I was with nobody home in my house, and neither of my two neighbors home, and the four ugly cats in apartment 3D yowling away. I felt lonely and very scared. This had seldom ever happened to me before. I flopped down in front of my apartment, 3B, and started crying. Maybe I was kind of loud, because soon Mr. Freeman opened his door.

"Why are you making all that noise?" he shouted.

"Because I forgot my key." I sniffled. "And Mrs. Hernandez and Mr. Kaspian are not home."

"Well, stop that racket! Right now!" He slammed his door very loud.

I went right on crying. But not so loud. It must have been loud enough, because after awhile, Mr. Freeman opened his door again.

"Didn't I tell you to stop that noise?" he bellowed. "And where's your mother, anyway?"

"She's working," I told him. "And she won't be home until six. So I'll have to sit here until she comes home, because I forgot my key, and Mrs. Hernandez—"

"I know, I know. You told me." But this time he didn't slam his door. He stood there, watching me. "So what would Mrs. Hernandez do for you and that loudmouth, Kaspian, if they were home?"

"They would let me wait in their apartment. Mrs. Hernandez would give me cookies and milk." I sniffed. "Mr. Kaspian would tell me to watch TV."

"He never turns it off," Mr. Freeman said. "He plays it so loud, I can't get any rest." He continued to stand in his doorway and watch me cry.

"All right! All right! Stop that racket!" he finally said in a cranky voice. "You can come inside and wait here. Come on. But don't bother my cats!"

I stopped crying and jumped right up. Nobody on our floor had ever gone into Mr. Freeman's apartment. I picked up my backpack and followed him inside.

I could hear the four cats yowling.

"I'm coming. I'm coming," he said, hurrying down the hall.

All four of them were waiting in the kitchen. They were standing beside four bowls of water and four empty bowls.

"This is when I feed them," Mr. Freeman said. "Every day at three-thirty sharp. Go sit over at the table, and don't scare them."

I sat on a chair full of cat hair and watched Mr. Freeman open four cans of cat food and dump the food into the four empty bowls. The cats stopped yowling and began eating.

"They're hungry," Mr. Freeman said, almost smiling.

"I'm hungry too," I told him. "Usually I have a snack when I come home from school."

"What do you eat?" Mr. Freeman asked, wrinkling up his ugly face. I saw him looking at the empty cans of cat food.

"Not cat food," I said. "I like cookies or apples or ice cream."

"I don't have cookies or apples or ice cream," he said.

"Well, I also like chips or candy or pretzels."

Mr. Freeman opened his refrigerator and looked inside. "I don't have chips or candy or pretzels."

I stood up and looked over Mr. Freeman's shoulder into his refrigerator. It was nearly empty except for a can of tomato soup, a few eggs, and some dried-up cheese. It didn't smell good.

"Never mind," I told him. "I'm not really hungry anymore."

I sat down again and watched the cats.

"I don't know," Mr. Freeman said, shaking his head. "I don't know what children like to eat. I never had any children."

"The cats like their food," I said.

Mr. Freeman closed the refrigerator door. "Except for him," he said, pointing to one of the cats, a black one. "He doesn't eat enough."

I looked at the black cat who seemed to me to be gobbling down his food faster than the others. "He's eating a lot today," I said.

"But he always leaves some over. And he's too skinny. I haven't had him as long as the others, and I'm still not sure what he likes to eat. I worry about him."

"Where did he come from?"

Mr. Freeman sat down on the one other chair at the table. He had a rough, wrinkled face with a big, red nose. "He's an alley cat. They all are. Each one of them. One by one, they showed up on my fire escape, and when I opened the window, they came in and never left. Except for him, the black one. He likes to go out. Sometimes he stays out for weeks. But this has been such a cold winter—the coldest one I remember in San Francisco. So he's been hanging around more. The important thing is he always comes back sooner or later. All of them know they have a home with me."

The black cat was the first one finished and, sure enough, he left some of his food in his bowl. He jumped up on Mr. Freeman's lap and glared at me out of one eye.

"He only has one eye," I said.

"That's right. Who knows how it happened, but you can be sure he hasn't had an easy time. Poor thing!" said Mr. Freeman in a very loving voice, stroking the cat who finally stretched out on his lap. Then, one by one, the other cats finished eating and jumped up into Mr. Freeman's lap also. He had room for all of them. "They're my family," said Mr. Freeman.

After that, I never had to stay in Mr. Freeman's apartment again. Either Mrs. Hernandez or Mr. Kaspian was home if I forgot my key. But Mr. Freeman used to nod if he passed me in the hall, and once he gave me a book. It was all about cats. I didn't bother reading it.

When Mr. Freeman died suddenly, everybody on our floor was surprised.

"The meanest man in the world!" said Mrs. Hernandez. "I figured he was going to live forever, he was so mean."

"I was just talking to him," said Mr. Kaspian. "To tell the truth, I was talking, and he was shouting. I was just telling him in a nice, calm voice that if he didn't stop his cats from yowling all night long, I was going to call the police. He started shouting. He called me names—I won't even repeat them. There was certainly nothing the matter with his lungs."

"Who?" said my mother. "I don't think I ever even saw him." My mother doesn't know any of the neighbors. She's never home because she works so many jobs.

Mr. Apple, the landlord, said that Mr. Freeman did not seem to have any family. "So," he said, "I'm going to call the S.P.C.A. right away and tell them to come and take away the cats."

"Good!" said Mr. Kaspian.

"Good!" said Mrs. Hernandez.

"Cats?" said my mother, sneezing. "I didn't realize anybody on this floor had cats."

"No!" I said to all of them. "Don't call the S.P.C.A. They'll take away the cats and kill them."

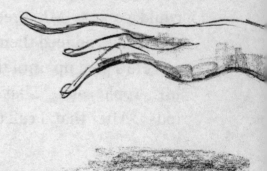

"Who cares?" said Mrs. Hernandez. "Nobody would want those cats. They're the ugliest, nosiest, meanest cats I ever saw."

"Just like Mr. Freeman," said Mr. Kaspian. "Especially that big, fat, orange one. He's the worst."

"But Mr. Freeman loved those cats," I told them. "They were like his family. It's not fair to kill them just because he's dead."

"Will you take them?" Mr. Apple asked.

"No!" said my mother, sneezing. "I'm allergic to cats. Absolutely not!"

"I guess not," I told Mr. Apple. "But I could go into Mr. Freeman's apartment every day and feed them."

"He's paid up until the first of March," Mr. Apple said. "That's three days from today. After that, I call the S.P.C.A."

So I had three days to find homes for four cats. But first, I had to feed them. Mr. Apple gave me the key to Mr. Freeman's apartment.

"There's nothing in there anybody would want," he said. "Some broken-down furniture, and a pile of old papers. You have three days."

Day One

First, I went to the closest grocery store, and asked the grocer what kind of cat food to buy. I bought the cat food she suggested with my own allowance. Then I let myself into Mr. Freeman's apartment. I could hear the cats even before I opened the door. They sounded angry.

All of them were waiting at the door with their mouths wide open and terrible noises coming out of them. When they saw it was me, they took off screeching and yowling.

Each of the four cats was ugly, all right.

One was big, fat, and orange.

One was short, fat, and a scuzzy white.

One was medium gray, fat, and had a raggedy tail.

And the ugliest of all was the skinny, black, one-eyed cat Mr. Freeman had worried about.

The orange one jumped up on top of the refrigerator, the scuzzy white one leaped on a pile of papers, the gray one backed up against the TV, and the black, one-eyed cat plastered himself against the window. All of them continued screeching and yowling.

"Don't be afraid," I told them. "I'm not going to hurt you."

The house was dusty, and smelled bad. There were papers piled up all over the living room and the kitchen. Under the sink, I found eight empty bowls. I filled four of them with cat food, and four of them with water.

"Come and eat," I called. But none of them did. They just kept on yowling.

So I left the apartment and stayed outside for twenty minutes. When I came back, all the food and water was gone. None of the cats were in sight. But I could hear them yowling.

"What am I going to do?" I asked out loud. "I have three days to find homes for four cats, and they're not only ugly, they're noisy and unfriendly."

I walked over to one of the windows and looked outside. We saw the same view from our living-room window. We shared the same fire escape over a street full of markets and people and buses.

It was stuffy in the apartment, so I opened the window. Suddenly, a furry black body flew by me, leaped down the fire escape, and into the street. He jumped up on one of the garbage cans down there and arched himself, hissing and glaring at me.

"Whew!" said a voice behind me. "It smells terrible in here. Whew!"

Mr. Kaspian stood behind me. "You should open all the windows," he said. "Air the place out."

He opened another window and then looked around him. "I've never been inside here," he said. "Twenty-three years I lived next door to him, and I've never been inside."

"I don't know what I'm going to do with the cats," I told Mr. Kaspian. "I don't want the S.P.C.A. to come and take them away."

"Nobody will want them," said Mr. Kaspian. "They're so ugly."

Suddenly the big, orange cat came into the room, yowling.

"Especially that one," said Mr. Kaspian. "He's the ugliest and the noisiest. Just listen to him. I'd know his yowling anywhere."

The big, orange cat hurried up to Mr. Kaspian and he rubbed himself against Mr. Kaspian's leg. The cat stopped yowling.

Mr. Kaspian pulled his leg away. "Why is he doing that?" he yelled.

"Maybe he thinks you're Mr. Freeman," I told him.

"He's pretty stupid if he does," said Mr. Kaspian.

The big, orange cat rubbed himself against Mr. Kaspian's other leg and, suddenly, made a sweet, purring sound.

"Just listen to that," said Mr. Kaspian. "Who would think such an ugly cat could make such a nice sound."

"I think he likes you," I said.

"Nobody likes me," said Mr. Kaspian. He sat down, and the orange cat immediately jumped up onto his lap.

"What's his name?" Mr. Kaspian wanted to know.

I didn't know his name. I didn't even know if any of the cats had names. But if you don't have a name, it's hard to get somebody to like you. And I wanted Mr. Kaspian to like this big, orange, ugly cat.

"Barney," I said. "His name is Barney."

"That's a funny name for a cat," said Mr. Kaspian. He put a hand on the cat's head, and Barney stretched out on his stomach, purring.

"I don't know anything about cats," said Mr. Kaspian. "I don't even know what they eat."

"The grocer knows," I told him. "She'll tell you."

DAY TWO

BEFORE SHE LEFT FOR WORK THE next day, my mother gave me a shopping list. It said, "One quart milk, one loaf bread, one package cheese, one bag potato chips, one bag corns chips, Froot Loops, three lemons, two frozen burritos, and a can of sardines."

"Yuck!" I told her. "I hate sardines."

"Well, I don't," she told me. "Make what you like for lunch, and don't leave your dishes in the sink."

I decided to go shopping first. For one thing, I needed some more cat food. I used to go to the big supermarket five blocks away, where everything is cheaper. But I liked the grocer in the little store, and I liked the way she'd suggested the cat food.

The grocer filled up two bags with my groceries, and gave me change. "Did your cats like the cat food I suggested?" she asked.

"They aren't my cats," I told her. "They belong to Mr. Freeman, who just died."

"Tsk! Tsk!" she said. "He was a very nice man."

"Nobody else thought so," I told her.

"He used to shop here all the time," said the grocer. "He always talked to me about his cats. He really loved them."

"Well, now, the landlord, Mr. Apple, wants to call the S.P.C.A. to come and take them away."

"Tsk! Tsk!" said the grocer.

"They aren't very beautiful cats," I told her. "So I don't think the S.P.C.A. will be able to find homes for them."

"Tsk! Tsk!" said the grocer. "Beauty isn't everything."

"They'll probably have to kill them."

"Tsk! Tsk!"

"I found a home for one of them yesterday. Now that the one-eyed black cat is back, I have three left, and only two days to go. Mr. Apple is planning on renting the apartment on the first of March. By the way, do you have a cat?"

"I used to," she said. "Her name was Lupe. She died on New Year's Day. She was very good at catching mice. Since she died, we've had lots of mice."

"Tsk! Tsk!" I said. "You need a new cat. One that's good at catching mice."

"I would take one," she said. "If it was really good at catching mice."

"I know just the one," I told her. "Her name is Barbie—one of Mr. Freeman's cats. She's very good at catching mice." I really didn't know if she was. And I don't know why I said her name was Barbie. But why not? None of the two remaining cats had names yet.

"And I wouldn't want one of those quiet, crazy cats that sneaks up on you," said the grocer.

"Believe me, Barbie is not quiet."

"And what's your name?" she asked me.

"Lily. What's yours?"

"Mrs. Rios," said Mrs. Rios. "I tell you what, Lily, why don't you bring Barbie over here today. We'll see how she fits in."

The three cats were waiting at the door, and scattered, yowling, as soon as I came into the apartment. But this time, they all stayed in the hall, watching me as I filled their bowls with food and water. And this time, they eased themselves into the kitchen, keeping an eye on me as I pressed myself against the farthest wall. They gobbled up their food, and drank their water, and hissed and yowled at me in between. I gave them all their names.

"You are Barbie, " I told the gray one, "after the doll."

"And you are Dolly," I said to the scuzzy white one, "after the singer."

"And you," I told the black, one-eyed cat, "are Leonardo, after the actor."

"I have just found a home for you, Barbie," I told her. "All we have to do is take you over to meet your new owner."

Which was easier said than done.

Barbie scratched me when I tried to pick her up. She scratched Mr. Kaspian when he tried to put her into a box. And, finally, she ran underneath the bed in the bedroom, yowling and screeching. She would not come out.

That was when Mr. Apple came into the apartment with a mean-looking woman.

"This is the apartment that will be vacant the day after tomorrow," he told her. "It's a mess. You will have to clean it out, paint it, buy a new stove and refrigerator, and give me two months' rent in advance."

"I'll think about it," said the mean-looking woman. "Why is that cat making so much noise?"

"We're trying to get her out from under the bed, and she won't come."

The woman bent down by the side of the bed and began murmuring.

After awhile, Barbie came out from underneath the bed. The woman picked her up, patted her head, and put her into Mr. Kaspian's box. "Cats are not hard to understand," she said. "I have six of them."

"No cats!" said Mr. Apple. "I'm looking for a tenant who doesn't have cats."

"Then you can forget about me," said the woman. She looked around the apartment with her dark, beady eyes. She narrowed them when she saw the piles of papers underneath Dolly.

She looked like a witch.

"It's too dark in here," she said. "I wouldn't take this place even if you lowered the rent, cleaned out all the garbage, and did the painting."

"Ha! Ha!" said Mr. Apple.

"I'm going," she said.

"So go!" said Mr. Apple.

"I'm glad she isn't taking the apartment," I told Mr. Kaspian after Mr. Apple left. "She looked like a witch."

"Six cats are too many," said Mr. Kaspian. He handed me a box with Barbie yowling inside.

"Two to go," I told him.

DAY THREE

BARBIE WAS ASLEEP IN THE WINDOW of the grocery store when I arrived the next morning.

"She made herself right at home," said Mrs. Rios. "I guess she likes it here."

"Did she catch any mice yet?" I asked.

Mrs. Rios shrugged her shoulders. "She just got here," she said. "What's the hurry? But Lily, I like her very much. And she's such a beautiful cat."

I took another look at Barbie. She looked just as ugly asleep as she did awake.

Mrs. Rios was patting her own head. "And we both have the same color gray hair."

I only had to buy two cans of cat food. Tomorrow, if I didn't find homes for the two remaining cats, I wouldn't have to buy any. I put the key into Mr. Freeman's door lock, but it didn't turn. The door was unlocked. Maybe Mr. Apple was showing the apartment to someone else. Slowly, I opened the door. It was not Mr. Apple. A woman was standing right there in the middle of the living room with her back toward me.

She moved toward the pile of papers on which Dolly sat. A bony hand reached out. . . .

"What are you doing here?" I yelled.

She spun around. I saw the same, mean-looking, witchy woman I had seen yesterday. She glared at me out of her small, gleaming eyes. "Who are you?" she demanded.

"I'm a neighbor," I told her. "I saw you here yesterday when Mr. Apple showed you the apartment. He said you couldn't live here with your six cats."

"I wouldn't want to live here in this dump, anyway," she said in a raspy voice. She turned again toward the pile of papers. "Go away, now," she said. "Mind your business."

"I'm the only other person who has the key," I told her. "How did you get in?"

She didn't answer but, again, put out a creepy hand toward the pile of papers.

"What is it you want?" I demanded. "Is there something in that pile of papers?"

"What's going on here?" Mr. Apple stood in the doorway. "And why are you back?"

"I forgot something," the witchy woman muttered. And then, lowering her head, she ran out of the apartment.

"I don't know how she got in," I told Mr. Apple. "I thought nobody else had the key except for you and me."

"Maybe you left the door open," Mr. Apple said. "I wonder what she left here."

"I don't think she left anything," I told him. "But she was very interested in that pile of papers Dolly is sitting on."

"Who?"

"The cat. She's sitting on a pile of papers. Do you think there might be something valuable in there?"

Mr. Apple looked at his watch. "Some people are coming to look at the apartment. Any minute now. I was going to tell them they'd have to get rid of the papers, but maybe we should have a look . . . just in case."

"Maybe he hid some money in there."

Mr. Apple hurried toward the pile of papers. "Here, get down! Get away!" he shouted at Dolly.

She jumped down and ran into the kitchen, where Leonardo was waiting. For me. Near his dish. I filled his and Dolly's dishes with food, and then I filled two other dishes with water. I could hear Mr. Apple grunting as he began looking through the papers.

"Here, you, Lily, give me a hand," he called out.

I returned to the living room. Mr. Apple was sitting on the floor with papers all around him.

"You know how to read, don't you? Just start looking through these papers. If you find anything valuable, I'll give you . . . I'll give you . . ."

"There are a lot of papers," I told him. "Not only in here, but in the kitchen, the bedroom, and even in the bathtub."

"Five dollars," he said, turning an old magazine upside down and shaking it.

"No," I said. "I don't want five dollars."

"Ten," he said. "I'll give you ten. But only if you find something valuable."

"I don't want ten, either," I said. "I want something else."

"What?" He was impatiently turning the pages of yellowed newspaper. "What do you want?"

"Another few days," I told him. "At least another two days. So I can find homes for the two cats."

"One day," said Mr. Apple. "You can have tomorrow. It turns out that tomorrow is the twenty-ninth of February, anyway. This is leap year. So Mr. Freeman is paid up through tomorrow. Now, get busy!"

The rest of the day, Mr. Apple and I went through every pile of paper we could find. Different people showed up to look at the apartment. They all swore they didn't have pets. Mr. Apple decided to give the apartment to two old ladies who paid him two months' rent. They said they would like to send in a cleaning crew the next day.

"The day after," I told them.

The cats watched us as we worked. Dolly moved from her seat on one pile of papers to another. Leonardo sat pressed up against the fire escape window. But the cats kept yowling.

"Night and day. Day and night," said Mr. Apple, looking into some big, white, empty envelopes. "They never stop yowling. I don't know how he could stand it. Thank goodness the new tenants won't have any pets. Whew, it's stuffy! Open the window, Lily, get a little air in here."

It was raining outside. But I opened the fire-escape window, and Leonardo went scampering down the slippery, gray fire escape.

"Mr. Freeman said Leonardo likes to go out," I told Mr. Apple. "I guess the weather doesn't always stop him."

"And sometimes he stays out all night." Mr. Apple flipped through a big, fat catalog. "But he never stops yowling. Lots of nights I don't get any sleep because of him. I'll be glad when he's gone."

"I won't," I said.

We spent the rest of the day looking through the piles of paper. As different people continued to come look at the apartment, I asked all of them if they wanted a cat. Nobody did. At the end of the day, only one small pile of papers remained in the bathtub.

"A whole day wasted," said Mr. Apple.

"Not completely wasted," I told him. "You found two brand-new wallets."

"With nothing in them."

"A coupon good for one giant-sized pizza at Pizza Heaven."

"You can have it."

"An army dog tag."

"You can have that, too."

"Three photograph albums of people we don't know."

"This was your idea," he said. "I wasn't going to bother."

"One last pile in the bathtub," I said. "And then we're all through."

Mr. Apple waved his hand at me. "I'm through. Right now. If he had anything valuable, he wouldn't have hid it in a pile of papers in the bathtub."

Mr. Apple stood up. Not exactly straight. His back was stooped from all that bending. "I'm going downstairs. You can look, if you're stupid enough. I'm finished."

"But, remember, Mr. Apple, you said I could have tomorrow. Remember? You promised."

"I remember! I remember! Just make sure to lock the door when you leave tonight. I don't want that old witch getting in again."

It took me another half an hour to go through the last pile of papers. It was no different from the others—old newspapers, magazines, catalogs, letters, cards, pictures . . .

There was nothing valuable. Or if there was, only the old, witchy woman would know. All I knew was that I had one more precious day to find homes for Dolly and Leonardo.

FEBRUARY 29

BEFORE LETTING MYSELF INTO Mr. Freeman's apartment to feed the cats, I knocked at Mr. Kaspian's door.

"Who's there?" he called out.

"It's me, Lily."

Mr. Kaspian looked at me through his peephole. Then he unlocked the three locks on his door and opened it. "Come in, Lily. Come in," he said.

Barney was stretched out on the old faded sofa in Mr. Kaspian's living room. He lifted a lazy head as I came into the room, but then laid it down again, and closed one eye.

"He just ate," Mr. Kaspian said. "He has a very good appetite."

"He's not making any noise," I said. "How come he's not making any noise?"

"Maybe he's happy here," said Mr. Kaspian.

"I'm sure he's happy," I told Mr. Kaspian. "Why shouldn't he be?"

Mr. Kaspian sat down carefully next to Barney. He scratched Barney's head. Barney opened the one closed eye and made a sweet, purring sound in his throat.

"It's nice having a pet," said Mr. Kaspian. "You always have company when you have a pet."

"Well, that's what I wanted to talk to you about, Mr. Kaspian. I was wondering if you might want to take another one of the cats. Maybe Leonardo?"

Mr. Kaspian shook his head.

"Or maybe Dolly?"

"One is enough for me," said Mr. Kaspian. "Why don't you ask Mrs. Hernandez?"

"I did," I told him. "But she said she has enough to do taking care of Mr. Hernandez. She doesn't want any more mouths to feed."

"Mr. Apple, maybe?"

"He hates cats," I said. "Besides, he's not talking to me right now. I don't know what to do, Mr. Kaspian. This is my last day. Tomorrow Mr. Apple is going to call the S.P.C.A."

"You'll think of something, Lily," said Mr. Kaspian.

"But what?" I asked myself as I put the key into Mr. Freeman's lock. Again, it didn't turn.

I opened the door, and there she was again.

"How did you get in?" I demanded.

"The door was open," she said. "What happened here?"

The papers lay scattered all over the floor where we had left them yesterday.

"We went through all the papers," I told her. "There wasn't anything valuable in them."

"Why should there be?" she asked.

"Because I saw you looking at them. At the papers. You thought there was something valuable in them, didn't you?"

"Valuable?" she repeated, narrowing her eyes at me.

"Yes, I saw you looking at the papers. There was something valuable in them, wasn't there?"

She began laughing suddenly—a dry, creaking laugh. Her mouth stretched out across her teeth.

It was scary, but I was determined. "Wasn't there?" I insisted.

"Very funny," she said, laughing even harder. "Something valuable in the papers! Oh, my!"

"We spent the whole day going through those papers, and Mr. Apple didn't think it was so funny. And neither do I. This is my last day, and if I don't find homes for the two cats, he's going to call the S.P.C.A., and they'll take them away."

She stopped laughing. "Where are the cats?" she snapped.

It was very quiet in the apartment. Where were they, anyway?

"I'll put out their food," I told her. "They'll come when I put out their food."

Sure enough, even before I filled their bowls with food and water, the two of them streaked into the kitchen from the bedroom.

"Maybe they were hiding under the bed," I said. "Maybe they were scared of you."

"I don't think so," she said, watching them eat. "Cats are never scared of me."

That's when I thought of something, as Mr. Kaspian said I would.

"Maybe you'd like to take them," I said. "I know you have six cats, and Mr. Apple won't let you come here. But maybe you can find another place where the landlord doesn't mind cats. There isn't much difference between six cats and eight."

"Seven," she said. "I'll take one cat. I'll take that one." She pointed at Dolly.

"That one's Dolly. But Leonardo is very nice, too, even though he only has one eye. Why don't you take him, too?"

"I don't want him," she said.

When Dolly finished eating, the witchy woman murmured something to her and picked her up. Dolly immediately nestled against her shoulder.

"Please!" I said to the woman. "Please, take Leonardo. Mr. Apple will call the S.P.C.A. tomorrow if I can't find a home for him. Please!"

The woman hesitated. She looked at me, and then she looked at Leonardo. She whispered something to him. He hissed at her, arched his back, and tore across the living room. Then he leaped up on the sill of the fire-escape window and plastered himself against it.

"He doesn't want to come with me," she said. "Don't worry about the S.P.C.A. Just open the window. It's a nice, sunny day and he knows how to take care of himself, anyway."

She began moving across the room with Dolly tucked under her ear.

"But won't you tell me before you go what you were looking for in Mr. Freeman's papers? Won't you tell me what was so valuable in those papers?"

"Yes, I will tell you," she said, smiling at me. Suddenly, she didn't look mean or witchy. "You are a good girl, and I owe you a favor. You were right. There was something valuable."

"In the papers?"

"Not exactly. Not *in* the papers. *On* the papers."

"*On* the papers?"

"Yes. *On* the papers. It was the cat you call Dolly, sitting on the papers. She's a very, very rare cat. A Tibetan Temple cat. There are very few in this country. A cat like this with her special markings is worth thousands of dollars."

"But how did Mr. Freeman get her?"

"I don't know. But I have her now. I could sell her, but I probably won't."

"Thousands of dollars? Mr. Apple will be very angry."

"I wouldn't tell him, then." She paused in the doorway, looking at Leonardo pressed against the fire-escape window.

"Open the window," she said, and left.

NOW I'M ELEVEN. A WHOLE YEAR has passed since Mr. Freeman died.

The two old ladies who live in apartment 3D are very neat. They wash their windows once a week, and Mrs. Hernandez says they're crazy. "There's a limit to how clean anybody should be," says Mrs. Hernandez. But they're not mean or ugly or loud. Whenever I forget my key, I can ring their bell in case Mrs. Hernandez or Mr. Kaspian aren't home. They always let me come in, and give me gingersnaps and tea if I'm hungry. Then they sweep the floor around where I'm sitting in case I've dropped any crumbs.

I see Barney whenever I visit Mr. Kaspian. He's grown fatter and lazier. Mr. Kaspian says he's grown fatter and lazier, too. I can't see any difference in him except he smiles more, and he never argues with the two ladies in 3D.

I see Barbie even more often. Every day, when I go past the store, there she is in the window.

"Business has really improved," Mrs. Rios says. "I think people like to see Barbie sitting in the window. She's such a pretty cat, too. She lights up the whole store. Who cares if she doesn't catch mice? I can always call the exterminator whenever it gets too bad."

Barbie doesn't seem very pretty to me. Mr. Kaspian says it's love that makes Mrs. Rios think Barbie is pretty. "That's why they say, 'Love is blind,'" he says. But then he'll go on to say Barney is really a beautiful cat. So, I suppose, love works the same way for him, too.

I never see Dolly. I looked in the cat book Mr. Freeman gave me for a picture of a Tibetan Temple cat. It didn't have one. So I went to the library, and the librarian showed me a book that had a picture of a Tibetan Temple cat. It was a beautiful cat, and as far as I could see, Dolly didn't look anything like that picture. But I have a feeling she's happy with her new owner and the six other cats, wherever she is.

I feel good when I think of the homes I found for those three cats. For a while, I didn't feel so good about Leonardo. Especially when I heard him yowling outside Mr. Freeman's window. Only Mr. Freeman did not live there anymore, and the two ladies never open that window. They always have the shade pulled down and they say it's dangerous to keep a fire escape window open. They say I should make sure always to close my window, too. We are on the same fire escape.

I have to keep that window closed most of the time, too. My mother is so allergic to cats, she wouldn't stop sneezing if Leonardo ever came into our apartment. But I can fill a bowl with water and another one with cat food whenever he does come. And I can sit outside on the fire escape with him while he eats, and keep him company. Lately, he's been stretching out on my lap after he finishes eating, and he lets me stroke his head. I like sitting out there with him, looking over the markets down below, and making believe he's my cat. But he's not. He's nobody's cat. And after awhile, he gets up and runs off down the fire escape.

Sometimes I don't see him for weeks and weeks. Then suddenly, there he is yowling outside my window. Maybe he hangs around a few days, and then Mr. Apple threatens to call the S.P.C.A. "All night long," Mr. Apple says, "he keeps on yowling. Why doesn't he just go away and stay away?" But Mr. Apple never does call the S.P.C.A. He knows how I feel about Leonardo even if he never says so.

I miss Leonardo when he's gone, but I don't worry about him the way Mr. Freeman did. I know Leonardo can take care of himself. His home is wherever he is. Maybe there is another girl who puts out food and water for him on her fire escape. Maybe a man like Mr. Freeman who welcomes him into his home. But I know that he likes me best. Even though he's still skinny, and only has one eye, I think he's the most beautiful cat of all of them.

I'm glad Mr. Freeman was nice to me once.

BARNEY

BARBIE

DOLLY

LEONARDO